Martin's Mice

Babe: The Gallant Pig
Harry's Mad

Martin's Mice

Dick King-Smith

Illustrations by Jez Alborough

Crown Publishers, Inc.
New York

Published in 1989 in the United States of America by
Crown Publishers, Inc., a Random House company,
225 Park Avenue South, New York, New York 10003.

First published in 1988 in Great Britain by Victor Gollancz Ltd.

CROWN is a trademark of Crown Publishers, Inc.
Manufactured in the United States of America

Library of Congress Cataloging-in-Publication Data

King-Smith, Dick.
Martin's mice / by Dick King-Smith;
illustrations by Jez Alborough.
p. cm.
Summary: A farm cat who doesn't want to catch mice
keeps a family of them as pets in the barn; but then
he is given away to a townswoman and acquires
a new perspective.
[1. Cats—Fiction. 2. Mice—Fiction.] I. Alborough, Jez, ill.
II. Title
PZ 7.K5893Mar 1989
[Fic]—dc19 88-20359
ISBN 0-517-57113-7

10 9 8 7 6 5 4 3 2

Contents

I

What a dear little thing!

"Mercy! Mercy!" cried the mouse.

It felt like a rather fat mouse, and when Martin took his paw off it, he could see that indeed it was.

"Oh, dear!" he said. "I'm most awfully sorry!"

Even when the farm kittens were very young, not long after their eyes first opened in their nest in an old hay-filled wooden crib, the mother cat, whose name was Dulcie Maude, had known that Martin was different from his brother, Robin, and his sister, Lark. (Dulcie Maude, as you can see from her choice of names, was fond of small birds.)

Robin and Lark soon began to have play fights, leaping upon one another from ambush and pretending to tear out each other's throat with fierce little squeaky growls. But Martin did not like the rough stuff and would hide behind his mother. And when

Dulcie Maude first brought home a very small mouse for the growing kittens, Martin wouldn't touch it. He watched his brother and sister as they worried at the tiny gray body, but he would not join in.

"Aren't you going to try a bit, Martin?" said his mother. "Mice are nice, you know. What's the matter?"

"It was so pretty," whispered Martin. "Poor little thing."

"Don't be such a wimp," said Robin with his mouth full.

"You're just a scaredy-cat," said Lark.

"I quite agree," said Dulcie Maude sharply.

"Whoever heard of a cat that didn't like mice!" And she gave Martin a spank. "Now start eating and stop being so silly!"

Somehow Martin managed a mouthful of mouse. Then he went into a corner and was sick.

And so it went on. Dulcie Maude brought home more and bigger mice, and, being a no-nonsense mother, insisted that Martin always eat a bit of mouse before he be allowed any of the kinds of canned meat that the farmer's wife put out for the cats. All of these—chicken or liver or fish flavored—Martin liked, but he was made to finish his mouse meat first, and though he learned to keep it down, he could not learn to enjoy it.

Luckily Robin and Lark always took the lion's share, shoving their wimpish brother out of the way, and at last the day dawned when Dulcie Maude dumped a final mouse in front of the kittens and said in her brisk way, "Now, then, I've worn my claws to the bone catching mice for you all, and you're quite big enough now to hunt for yourselves. You're on your own. See you around."

Robin and Lark were delighted. It was exciting to think of themselves as real hunters, and in barn and byre they stalked their prey or lay in wait and soon met with success.

Martin was delighted too. It meant that he need

never again eat mouse. Pretty little things! he mused. They shall not suffer because of me. I shall never catch one.

But though his intentions were good, his instincts, handed down to him by generations of expert mousers, were too strong, and he caught the very first mouse he met.

At the time, he was exploring in a loft over an old cart-shed. In the days that followed after his mother had left the kittens to their own devices, Martin had done a lot of exploring. Unlike the others who were busy hunting, he had plenty of time to wander around the farm. Already he had learned a number of lessons that a farm kitten needs to know. Cows have big feet

that could easily squash you, sows get angry if you go too near their piglets, broody hens are bad-tempered birds, and collie dogs chase cats.

Humans, Martin was glad to find, didn't chase cats. The farmer paid little attention to him, but the farmer's wife made sure he had enough to eat, and the farmer's daughter actually made quite a fuss of him, picking him up and cuddling him. One day she took Martin to see her rabbits, three white rabbits with pink eyes, that she kept in three large hutches at the bottom of the garden. Why did she keep them? he wondered.

The next time that Martin met his mother on his journeys, he asked her about this.

"Mother," he said. "Why does that girl keep those rabbits?"

"As pets," Dulcie Maude said.

"What's a pet?"

"A pet is an animal that humans keep because they like it. They like looking after it, feeding it, stroking it, making a fuss of it."

"So we're pets, are we?"

"Strictly speaking, I suppose. Dogs certainly are, always fussing around humans, sucking up to them."

"What about cows and pigs and sheep?"

"No, they're not pets," said Dulcie Maude. "Humans eat them, you see."

"But they don't eat cats and dogs?"

"Of course not."

"And they don't eat rabbits?"

"Yes, they eat rabbits. But not *pet* rabbits."

"Why not?"

As with most mothers, there was a limit to Dulcie Maude's patience.

"Oh, stop your endless questions, Martin!" she snapped. "Curiosity, in case you don't know, killed the cat!" And she stalked off, swishing her tail.

It was curiosity, nevertheless, that led Martin to climb into the cart-shed loft to see what was in it. What was in it, in fact, was a load of junk. The farmer never threw anything away in case it should come in handy one day, and the loft was filled with boxes of this and bags of that, with broken tools and disused harnesses and worn-out coats and empty tins and bottles that had once contained sheep dip or cow drench or horse liniment.

Against one wall stood an old white enameled bathtub with big brass taps and clawed cast-iron feet, and it was while Martin was exploring beneath it that something suddenly shot out.

Automatically, he put his paw on it.

"I'm most awfully sorry!" he said again, but the fat mouse only continued to say, "Mercy! Mercy!" in a quavery voice. It seemed to be rooted to the spot, and it stared up at Martin with its round black eyes as though hypnotized.

How pretty it looks, thought Martin. What a dear little thing!

"Don't be frightened," he said.

"It is not for myself alone that I beg you to spare me," said the mouse. "You see, I am pregnant."

What a strange name, thought Martin. I've never heard anyone called that before.

"How do you do?" he said. "I am Martin."

What a dear little thing, he thought again. I'd like to look after it, to feed it, to stroke it, to make a fuss of it, just as Mother said that humans like to do with their pets. After all, he thought, some humans eat rabbits but some keep them as pets. So in the same way, some cats eat mice, but some . . .

"Shall I tell you what I'm going to do with you?" he said.

"I know what you're going to do," said the mouse wearily. "After you've finished tormenting me, you're going to eat me."

"You're wrong," said Martin.

He bent his head and gently picked up the mouse in his mouth. Then he looked about him. He climbed onto an old wooden chest that stood handily beside the bathtub and looked down into its depths.

The perfect place, he thought excitedly. My little mouse can't escape—the plug's still in the drain and the sides are much too steep and slippery—but I can jump in and out easily. And he jumped in and laid his burden carefully down.

The mouse lay motionless. Its eyes were shut, its ears drooped, its coat was wet from the kitten's mouth.

"Shall I tell you what I'm going to do?" said Martin again.

"Kill me," said the mouse feebly. "Kill me and be done."

"Not on your life!" said Martin. "I'm going to keep you for a pet!"

2

You must be stupid

The mouse did not reply. It lay on the rust-stained bottom of the bathtub, shivering.

"Oh, dear, you're cold!" said Martin, and he began to lick the mouse with his warm tongue. But this only made it shudder violently, so he leaped out of the bathtub and began to look about the loft for something that would serve as bedding for his new pet.

First he found a piece of felt about a foot square, an offcut from the underlay of an old discarded carpet, and he managed to jump back into the tub with the felt in his mouth. He laid it down and put the mouse carefully on it. Leaping out again, Martin began to collect mouthfuls of straw from the stuffing of an old horse collar, packing it around the fat mouse to make a nest. Its eyes were open again, he noticed when he had finished, but it seemed to have lost its tongue, for when Martin said, "Comfy now?" it did not answer.

At any rate, it stopped shivering, he thought. Now I'd better get it some food.

He was halfway across the farmyard when it occurred to him that he did not know what mice ate. I can't ask Mother, he thought, or Robin or Lark. They mustn't know about my mouse.

He looked around and saw a sheep, peering through the bars of the yard gate from the field beyond. Sheep, he knew—because Dulcie Maude had told the kittens—were pretty thick, but maybe this one would know. He padded over to it and said politely, "Can you help me?"

"You?" said the sheep.

"Yes."

"Can I help you?"

"Yes."

"No," said the sheep.

"But you don't know what I was going to say next," said Martin.

The sheep appeared to be considering this. It was chewing its cud, and its lower jaw went steadily round and round with a crunching noise. Its yellow eyes looked quite mad.

"How can I know what you're going to say next?" it said at last. "What do you think I am—a mind reader?"

"No!" said Martin. "No, I certainly don't."

The sheep, which had a long sad face, looked disappointed at this, so Martin hastened to comfort it.

"But I'm sure," he said, "that you know all about mice and what they like to eat."

"Mice?" said the sheep.

"Yes."

"Field mice?"

"No, house mice."

"I don't know anything about house mice," said the sheep. "How could I? I don't live in a house. I live in a field."

"So you know about field mice?"

"No," said the sheep. "Do you?"

"No," said Martin.

"Then you're stupid," said the sheep, and walked away.

Martin made his way to the cowshed. Cows, he knew—because Dulcie Maude had told the kittens—were a bit brighter than sheep, and he walked along the low wall that separated the standings from the hay-filled feeding passage behind until he came to a cow that looked reasonably sensible.

Martin decided upon a more direct approach.

"Do you know what a mouse eats?" he said.

The cow's chain rattled as the big animal stretched out her muzzle to sniff at the kitten. She blew a snort of sweet, warm cow breath at him.

"Grass is nice," she said.

"For a mouse?"

"For cows," she said.

"Yes, yes," said Martin, "but do you know what a mouse eats?"

The cow appeared to be thinking deeply. She rolled her eyes and fluttered her long pale eyelashes.

"Look at it this way," she said after a while. "All cows are animals. Right?"

"Right."

"And all cows eat grass."

"Yes."

"Well, then. All mice are animals, so it follows that all mice eat grass."

"But that doesn't make sense," Martin said. "All cats are animals, but all cats don't eat grass."

"No," said the cow. "All cats eat mice."

"I don't," said Martin.

"That doesn't make sense either," said the cow. "You must be stupid." And she turned her head away and began a conversation with her neighbor.

Martin sighed. I'll ask a pig, he thought. He knew—because Dulcie Maude had told the kittens— that of all the farmyard animals, the pig is by far the cleverest. He made his way down to the pigsties.

He jumped up onto the wall of the first sty and

looked down. Beneath him lay a large boar. He was fast asleep and snoring, his mouth partly open. Martin noted the size of his tusks and judged that he had better mind his p's and q's. For all he knew, pigs ate cats. Flattery would do no harm, he thought, so he gave a little cough and, when the boar opened an eye, said in a buttery voice, "My mother tells me that of all the farmyard animals, the pig is by far the cleverest."

The boar levered himself to his feet.

"Indubitably," he said.

Martin did not know the meaning of this long word, but it seemed that the pig was not displeased, so he pressed on.

"So I'm sure you'll be able to tell me," he said, "what mice eat. I asked a sheep and I asked a cow, but neither of them knew."

"Predictably," said the boar. "The intelligence quotient of the average herbivore is abysmal. Carnivores, such as yourself, are a little better endowed, but in general it is the omnivores whose intellectual abilities are preeminent. Among the omnivorous creatures we find the humble mouse—possibly the exception that proves the rule—but far superior to all others are the pig and man. In that order."

The boar paused for breath.

Martin, half drowned in the sea of words, sat silent

and bemused for a moment. Then he said, "But I still don't see what mice eat."

The boar gave a loud grunt.

"To say that you are stupid," he said, "would be the understatement of all time." And he lay down again and shut his eyes.

There's only one thing for it, thought Martin. I'll have to go back and ask my little mouse what mice

eat. I can't waste any more time. She'll be very hungry by now.

He jumped off the pigsty wall and set off for the cart-shed. On the way he saw the farmer's daughter in the distance, and seeing her made him think of her rabbits. Dulcie Maude had said nothing to the kittens about the intelligence of rabbits, but perhaps it might be worth asking them. He jumped over the garden wall and ran down to the rabbit hutches. Three pairs of pink eyes stared blankly out at him. They don't look terribly clever, Martin thought. I shall speak clearly and slowly to them.

"What . . . do . . . mice . . . eat?" he said.

"Stick around," said the rabbits sourly, "and you'll soon see."

Martin stuck around, and before long a mouse appeared from nowhere, climbed the leg of the wooden trestle on which the hutches stood, popped in through the wire front of one of them, shoved its nose into the feeding bowl, and proceeded to gobble away with gusto.

"Oh, great!" cried Martin. "Mice eat rabbit food!"

"If you think that's great," said the rabbits (and they in their turn spoke clearly and slowly), "you . . . must . . . be . . . stupid."

3

What a jolly name!

Martin paid no attention to this remark because he was too busy thinking. He had discovered what mice ate, but how could he get hold of some of the stuff? Where was it kept?

At that very moment he heard footsteps coming down the garden path. The mouse that was eating the rabbit food heard them too and slipped out and away, as Martin went to meet the farmer's daughter and rubbed himself against her legs.

They both spoke at once. He heard a babble of sound as she said, "What do you want, kitty?" and she heard a mewing noise as he said, "Where do you keep the rabbit food?"

But then both questions were answered as the girl bent down and pulled out a large cookie tin from beneath the trestle and took off the lid. She opened one of the hutch doors and reached in to take out a feeding bowl, and while her back was turned, Martin acted.

Quick as a flash, he shoved his face into the tin and took the biggest mouthful he could manage of the little brown rod-shaped rabbit pellets. Then, slowly so as not to draw attention to himself, he walked away up the path, out of the garden gate, and back into the farmyard.

Suddenly, to his horror, he saw his mother approaching. What if she should speak to him? He could not reply with his mouth jam-packed with rabbit food. He changed direction, to avoid her, but so did she, to meet him.

"Martin, my son!" said Dulcie Maude. "I've not seen you for ages. How are you getting on? Robin and Lark have become quite expert mousers. How about you? You were always such a fussy eater. Have you caught one yet?"

Despite his bulging cheeks, Martin somehow managed a kind of strangled purr that must have sounded to Dulcie Maude like a "Yes," for she said, "Good. Good. You're looking much fatter in the face, I must say," and went on her way.

Martin waited till his mother was out of sight. Then he hurried to the cart-shed and climbed the flight of steps that led to the loft above. He leaped onto the wooden chest beside the bath and with great relief, for his jaws were aching, opened them to drop his burden.

"Look what I've brought you!" he cried with pride, but there was no reply. For a nasty moment Martin thought that his pet mouse had somehow escaped, but then he saw movement in the straw, which had now been neatly woven into a round ball. From a hole in the side of the nest ball a mouse appeared and began to feed hungrily upon the rabbit food.

But this was surely not his mouse! This was not the fat mouse with the strange name—"I am pregnant," it had said. But this was a thin mouse!

"Why," cried Martin in amazement, "you are not Pregnant!"

"Too true!" said the mouse, stuffing another rabbit pellet into its mouth and chewing busily.

"I don't understand you," said Martin.

The mouse regarded him beadily.

"I don't understand you," it said, "but thanks awfully for the grub. And you can have a peep if you like."

"A peep?"

"In the nest. Gently, mind."

Carefully, Martin jumped into the bath and scraped away a little of the straw on top of the nest ball.

Inside it, there were eight blind pink hairless baby mice.

"Oh!" gasped Martin. "Oh, I say! Aren't they lovely!"

"All thanks to you, Martin," said the mouse. "I've heard tell that a cat has nine lives, but you have spared that many—my life and my children's—and I am truly grateful."

"Oh, don't mention it!" said Martin in a fluster. "Don't mention it, um, er . . . "

"I'm afraid I confused you with regard to my name," said the mouse. "Actually, it's Drusilla."

"I say, what a jolly name!" said Martin.

The mouse went on busily eating, and Martin used this as an excuse to address her correctly.

"Is the food all right, Drusilla?" he said.

"Scrumptious," she said.

"And did I bring enough?"

"Enough for days!" said Drusilla. "Carried it in your mouth, I imagine?"

"Yes."

Drusilla licked her lips.

"I don't like to trouble you, Martin," she said, "when you've been so kind, but I *am* so terribly, terribly thirsty."

"Oh!" said Martin.

"I think it might be difficult," said Drusilla, "for you to transport water in the same way. So may I make a suggestion?"

"Of course, Drusilla," said Martin.

"If you were to put your paws in a puddle and then come straight back, there would be plenty of moisture on them. I only need a small amount. If you wouldn't object?"

"Of course not, Drusilla," said Martin. "I'll go straightaway. I won't be long."

Out in the yard, he looked for puddles, but the weather had been dry and warm and there were none. Martin felt rather relieved. Like all his kind, he hated getting his feet wet. But then he recalled that dear little voice saying, "I *am* so terribly, terribly thirsty."

The cattle trough was full, of course, but Martin was afraid of toppling in, so he made his way down to the duck pond. The water in it looked horribly wet, but Martin took his courage in both paws and gingerly dipped one in. Then cautiously, he waded in, while the ducks burst into fits of quacking laughter.

At this moment Robin and Lark appeared, walking one behind the other along the top of the wall that bounded the duck pond. They stopped opposite Martin and sat with their paws together and their tails curled neatly around them, looking down at him as he stood ankle deep in the water.

"Not only a wimp," said Robin.

"Not only a fool," said Lark.

"But . . ." they said, and Martin was waiting damply for them to call him what the sheep and the cow and the pig and the rabbits had called him, when there was a sudden loud barking. The farmer's black-and-white collie loved cat chasing, and Martin waited till his brother and sister had been chased a long way away. Then he waded out of the duck pond and made his way back to his pet. He did not like to go too fast, lest the water on his paws should all be shaken off, nor too slow, so giving it more time to run off, so he walked in a curious way, putting down each foot as carefully as though he were crossing thin ice.

At last he stood in the bathtub once more and dripped.

"Oh, cheers, Martin!" cried Drusilla, lapping eagerly at the drops of water as they ran off the kitten's legs onto the floor of the bathtub.

Martin jumped out onto the chest and sat cleaning his paws. He looked fondly over the rim at his little mouse, now well supplied with comfortable bedding and food and water, as a pet should be.

"Kids all right, Drusilla?" he said.

"Yes, they're fine, thanks," said Drusilla. "Everything's fine really, except for one thing."

"What's that?"

"Well," said Drusilla, "let's get things straight. You've made up your mind to keep me a prisoner, haven't you?"

"Not a prisoner. A pet. Just like the girl keeps her rabbits."

"Okay. I'm not grumbling. I'd much rather be your pet than your breakfast, which is what I would have been if you'd been an ordinary cat. But you know, Martin, pets like those rabbits don't only need bedding and food and water. There's something else that the girl has to do for the comfort of those rabbits, regularly."

"What's that, Drusilla?" said Martin.

"She has to clean them out, Martin. They're not house-trained, you know. And I," said Drusilla, "am not bath-trained."

4

Now I've got nine!

"Oh!" said Martin.

Oh, goodness, he thought, what's the answer to that?

Like all his kind, he was by nature particular about these matters. What's more, Dulcie Maude had given the kittens a thorough toilet training.

"When you want to go," she had said, "you find a patch of loose soil and you dig a little hole in it. Then, when you've finished, you cover it over with earth. All cats do this."

But I don't suppose all mice do, thought Martin, and anyway you can't dig holes in a tub.

Then suddenly his eye fell upon the drain plug. What's under a drain plug? A plug hole! Martin waited until Drusilla was safely back in her nest, nursing the babies, and then he dropped quietly into the tap end of the bath. There was even, he saw, a length of broken chain still attached to the plug, half a dozen little brass links fastened to the circle of soggy brown rubber.

He took them in his mouth and pulled.

For an instant Martin caught his breath. The drain hole was quite large enough for a mouse to go down through. Was he simply providing his pet with a way out? But then he peered into it and saw to his relief that it was barred by a little brass grating shaped like a cartwheel. To be sure, there were six holes in the grating, but they were too small for even the new thin Drusilla.

A means of escape it was not.

A perfect lavatory it was.

Just then Martin heard the nest straw rustle and found Drusilla at his elbow. Embarrassed, he wondered how to explain to her his solution to the problem of sanitation, but he need not have worried.

"Oh, goody!" said Drusilla. "The ladies' room!"

Now, as the weeks passed and the mouse cubs grew larger every day, it seemed, everything in the bath was lovely. By the time the cubs were two weeks old they had their teeth, and by three weeks they were keen to use them on solid food. Once they began to come out of the nest, smart in their first coats of silky gray hair, Drusilla set about bath-training them, and Martin set about providing for their healthy young appetites. Early on, Drusilla had explained something to him.

"What's 'omnivorous'?" he had asked her one day.

"Why?" said Drusilla.

"Somebody told me that mice are omnivorous," said Martin.

"So they are."

"But what does it mean?"

"It means that they eat anything and everything."

"Oh," said Martin.

"Like men do," said Drusilla.

"And pigs."

"Yes."

So now Martin fed his mice on a wide variety of choice foods. There was plenty to choose from on the farm. He stole dairy feed from the cows, and pig feed from the pigs, and sheep feed from the sheep. He took corn from the chickens and the ducks, and he took the bread crusts that the farmer's wife put out for the wild birds. A fallen apple that he found in the orchard lasted the family a long time, and, because it was juicy, satisfied their thirsts and saved Martin the need to paddle in the duck pond for a couple of days. Once he even brought a small mouthful of his own canned cat food (liver flavored), but Drusilla was quite sharp with him about that.

"Use your common sense, Martin," she said. "The children are much too young for such rich food. It will give them terrible tummy upsets." And she ate it herself.

But generally she was all sweetness and light, thanking Martin prettily for everything he brought and encouraging the cubs to do the same.

"What do you say, children?" she would ask when the kitten appeared with an offering, and eight squeaky little voices would answer, "Thank you, Uncle Martin."

Dear little things, thought Martin. Mouse-keeping really is the nicest hobby. And to think that I started with only one and now I've got nine! But even as he gazed fondly down at them all, he was dogged by a secret fear. Suppose one of the other cats should ever come up into the loft of the cart-shed? Nine would soon be none.

At that very moment he heard the scratch of claws on the flight of steps.

5

Was it a buck?

Robin! thought Martin. Or Lark! Or both! It's all over with my mice once they find them! They mustn't come up here. I must charge at them and knock them down the steps. It doesn't matter what they think, I must stop them!

He jumped off the wooden chest and dashed to the hole in the loft floor where the steps emerged. Climbing them, dimly seen in the gloom of the old windowless cart-shed, was an indistinct cat shape, and with a wild cry of "We'll see who's a wimp and a fool!" Martin launched himself at it. Together they tumbled to the floor. The next thing Martin felt was a terrific thump on one ear.

"You stupid boy!" hissed Dulcie Maude, thumping him on the other one. "Whatever do you think you're doing?"

"Oh, sorry, Mother!" gasped Martin. "I didn't know it was you."

"Well, you know now," said Dulcie Maude, and she gave him a third thump for luck. "Anyway," she said, "what in the world were you doing up in that loft? There are no mice up there, Martin. You should know by now that mice only live where there is food for them—in the cowsheds and the pigsties and the chicken houses. There's nothing for them to eat in that old loft, so there won't be any mice up there, will there?"

Martin did not reply.

"I saw you going into the cart-shed," went on Dulcie Maude, "so I followed you to see what you were up to, and the next thing I know you come hurtling down the steps, yelling some rubbish, and knock your poor old mother flying."

"Sorry, Mother," said Martin again. "I thought you were Robin. Or Lark. Or both. I was just playing. It was a game."

"Now look here, Martin," said Dulcie Maude briskly, "you're much too old to be playing silly games. Your job is to kill mice. Your brother and sister have got dozens. Why, yesterday they even clobbered a rat between them. So what about you, may I ask? How many mice have you got?"

"I've got nine, Mother," said Martin.

"Have you?" said Dulcie Maude. "Have you indeed?"

Like most mothers after they have walloped their children, she began to feel that maybe she'd been a bit hard on this odd son of hers. Kittens will be kittens, she thought, and she licked his nose.

"All right, Martin," she said in a kindly voice, "nine's not a bad score. But just you remember—you won't find any mice here."

"No, Mother," said Martin.

"You won't find Robin and Lark wasting their time in a place like this."

34

"No, Mother," said Martin.

"So don't waste yours. Be off with you now. A mouse a day," said Dulcie Maude, "keeps the vet away."

"Yes, Mother," said Martin. "I'll go and catch one now."

"On second thought," said Dulcie Maude, "I'll come with you."

"Oh," said Martin. "Oh, there's no need. I can manage."

"I daresay," said Dulcie Maude. "But I'd like to come along and watch you in action. Just to see if you're as good as the other two. We'll go to the chicken house. There are plenty of mice in there."

The hens were out foraging in the orchard, so the chicken house was empty except for one broody sitting in a nest, who fluffed her feathers with an angry squawk as the cats came in. Dulcie Maude settled herself comfortably in a patch of sunshine by the open door. Martin crouched beside a mouse hole in the far wall. The broody settled. All was quiet.

For a long time nothing moved. Both cats were still as statues. Only the dust motes danced in the sunlight shaft.

Dulcie Maude's eyes closed. She's asleep, thought Martin. Come out now, little mouse, and I'll make a

move and startle you and then you can run back into
your hole and Mother will never know.

As though it had read his mind, a mouse poked its
nose out. Just then a hen came in at the door on its
way to lay an egg and woke Dulcie Maude as the
mouse scurried out onto the henhouse floor. Martin
glanced at his mother out of the corner of his eye. She
was watching him.

I'll simply have to catch it, Martin thought. If I
miss it on purpose, she'll wallop me for starters and
then keep following me around till I do get one.

He tensed himself and leaped.

"Good boy!" said Dulcie Maude approvingly.

She rose and stretched herself.

"Bring it here," she said, "I could do with a snack."

Martin did not move.

"Martin!" said Dulcie Maude sharply. "Did you
hear what I said?"

Martin did not answer. He crouched, holding the
mouse between his forepaws (whose claws he had not
unsheathed), and faced his mother. He felt suddenly
very angry. First she pokes her nose into my loft,
then she beats me up, then she makes me catch a
mouse I don't want to catch, and now she wants it for
herself! She shan't have it!

He crouched lower, flattening his ears and swishing

his tail, and he growled the fiercest growl that he could manage.

"Well, well, well!" said Dulcie Maude. "How bloodthirsty we've grown!" She felt a mixture of maternal pride that the worm had turned and parental anger that it was a disobedient worm.

Martin growled again.

"Oh, keep your rotten mouse," said Dulcie Maude sniffily, and she turned and walked out of the chicken house.

Martin watched through the door till his mother was out of sight. Then he opened his paws.

"Scat!" he said.

"Scat?" said the mouse in a feeble voice.

"Yes," said Martin. "Make tracks! Beat it! Shove off! Scram!"

Dazedly the mouse got to its feet and staggered to its hole and crawled in.

"Was it a buck?" asked Drusilla when Martin told her the story later.

"A buck?"

"A male mouse. Male mice are bucks; females like me are does."

"I haven't a clue," said Martin. "I didn't ask. Why?"

"Oh, nothing," said Drusilla. "I just wondered."

6

It's boring!

Martin was curious. Why did it matter to Drusilla whether the mouse that he had caught was male or female? He thought about it for a while and then he said, "I think I've got it, Drusilla. If it had been a female, a doe, I mean, like you, you might have been pleased if I'd brought it home and then you could have had a friend?"

"Oh, don't be so stupid, Martin!" hissed Drusilla.

"You sound just like my mother," said Martin.

"I feel like your mother sometimes. You're so wet behind the ears that you make me mad!"

Martin put a paw behind each of his ears. They felt dry enough.

"Why are you so sharp with me?" he said.

"Because it's like having a ninth child," snapped Drusilla. "It's bad enough putting up with these eight big lumps."

"But don't you like your children?" asked Martin. "I think they're lovely."

By now the young mice were half as big as their mother. They had grown bold too and no longer called their keeper Uncle Martin. Two of them came rushing along the bottom of the tub, playing tag.

"Hi, Mart!" they cried as they dashed by.

"Of course I *like* them," said Drusilla angrily. "It's just that I'm fed up to the back teeth with the lot of them. If I were living a normal life instead of being cooped up in this lousy tub, I'd have kicked them out by now. 'You're on your own,' I'd have said to them. 'See you around.' As it is, they're driving me bananas. I never get a moment's peace. Can you wonder that I'm bad tempered?"

"Oh," said Martin.

He had grown very fond of Drusilla and did not like to see her upset.

"What do you want me to do?" he said.

"Let them go."

"Let them go! But then I'd only have one pet mouse instead of nine."

"You'd have one reasonably happy pet," said Drusilla, "instead of nine miserable ones," and she scurried into the old nest ball in a sulk.

"Drusilla!" said Martin. "Don't be like that!" But she would not answer.

Martin sat on the chest, frowning, watching the young mice. They didn't look miserable. They seemed to be having some sort of competition, each in turn taking a run and then jumping as high as it could up the steep sides of the bath. He was amazed how high they could jump for such little creatures, but each in turn fell short and slid down to the bottom again.

"What's the game, kids?" he said.

"It isn't a game, Mart," said one, and then all the rest began to chatter at him.

"We want to get out!"

"Out of this lousy tub!"

"We want to leave home!"

"And see the world!"

"And seek our fortunes!"

"Mum's fed up with us!"

"And we're fed up with her!"

"But don't you like it here?" said Martin. "Don't you like being my pets?"

"No!" they all squealed. "It's *boring!*"

"Oh," said Martin. "But if I let you out," he said, "you won't be safe, you know. My mother, now, or my sister and brother—they'll kill you."

"Oh, we know all about that, Mart," said one.

"Mum told us."

" 'Other cats are not like nice, kind Uncle Martin.' "

"If she's said that once, she's said it a hundred times."

"And we know all about mousetraps."

"And poison baits."

"And dogs."

"And men."

"Well, there you are," said Martin. "If I let you out, you're liable to die."

It's boring!

"We're liable to die of boredom if you keep us in," they squeaked, and once again they began their frantic jumping.

For the rest of the day Martin worried about the problem. The mouse cubs wanted to go. Drusilla wanted them to go. But they were so young, so little, so vulnerable. What should he do? He needed advice. From someone very clever. But who? The pig, thought Martin suddenly. I'll ask that pig. He made his way to the pigsties.

Underneath the wall of the first sty the great boar lay fast asleep and snoring, his mouth partly open, exactly as he had been when Martin first saw him. This time the kitten sat and waited patiently until at last the boar woke and looked up at him.

"Can I ask your advice?" said Martin.

The boar grunted. "It's the little ignoramus, isn't it?" he said.

"Actually," said Martin, "I'm a kitten."

The boar sighed. "Are you demented?" he said.

"No, I'm Martin."

The boar shook his head. "A martin," he said, "is a bird."

"We're all birds," said Martin. "My brother and my sister and me, we're all birds."

Once more, the big bristly boar levered himself to his feet.

"You will forgive me," he said, "if I seem anxious to terminate this fascinating conversation, but would you be good enough to come to the point? What is the subject upon which you need my counsel?"

"Well," said Martin, "it's like this. I've got eight young mice."

"Live ones?"

"Yes."

"Where?"

"In a bathtub."

"You have eight mice swimming in a bathtub of water?"

"No, it's an empty tub. What do you think I should do with them?"

"Had you not considered the possibility of devouring them? They would surely constitute an excellent repast."

"Sorry?" said Martin.

"Eat them," said the boar.

"But I don't eat mice," said Martin.

For a little while the boar stood silent, his head bowed, and stared at the ground. He looked the picture of someone carrying a heavy burden.

"If I were a mouse," he said at last slowly, "being kept in an empty tub by a cat who thinks he's a bird and, presumably for this reason, does not eat mice, I imagine that I should wish most fervently to be released before I went stark-raving mad."

"You mean you think I should let them out?" said Martin.

"Yes," said the boar.

So that night Martin did.

7

A big sleek dark one

Eight times Martin jumped into the bathtub, gently picked up one of Drusilla's children in his mouth, jumped out again, crept down the steps, and deposited the mouse cub on the floor of the cart-shed. To each in turn he made the same short speech.

"Listen carefully, kid," he said. "Take my advice. Get out of here. There's nothing to eat here. Go where the farmer keeps his animals—the cowsheds, the pigsties, the chicken house. That's where you'll find food. But whatever place you land up in, the first thing to do tonight is to find yourself a hole and get down it. Hens can peck you, cows can step on you, pigs will probably eat you if they get the chance. And so will the dog. And so, most certainly, will my mother or my brother or my sister. But none of them can get down a mousehole. So remember—first find a safe home and then you can go foraging. Off you go now, and the best of luck."

Confident as they had seemed in the comparative safety of the bath with their mother and Martin to look after them, some of the mouse cubs were now not so cocky as they bade farewell to the kitten. The boldest ones, to be sure, ran merrily off with loud cries of "So long, Mart, old bean! See you!" but others were more subdued as they made their way out of the cart-shed into the night. Indeed, the last to go, the smallest cub, was so nervous that it addressed the mouse-keeper with the politeness of babyhood.

"G-Good-bye, Uncle Martin," it said in a voice that trembled, and it paused in the doorway for a moment and looked back before it finally disappeared from sight.

Martin heaved a huge sigh. Dear little fellows! Would he ever see them again? Had he been right to

send them out into the harsh world? How would they manage? What would become of them?

How I shall miss them, he thought as he climbed back up the steps into the loft, and how much more will Drusilla!

"All gone!" he said to her sadly. "Try not to worry."

"Worry?" said Drusilla. "You must be joking. It's lovely to have the place to myself and the chance to tidy it up a bit. It's a mess. High time the bedding was changed, for a start, so don't just sit there, Martin, you can lend me a paw. Get rid of this musty old straw and then fetch me some fresh, and when you've done that, I'm dying for a drink and a square meal, so get a move on."

"Yes, Drusilla," said Martin.

The days that followed were relaxing ones for the kitten. Keeping one pet mouse was a great deal less trouble than providing for nine, and it was nice to have Drusilla to himself, without constant interruptions from the cubs, forever squabbling or demanding attention or asking silly questions.

"I can see now," he said, "why you were glad to see the back of them."

"I don't know what you mean," said Drusilla shortly.

"Well, you said they were driving you bananas. You said you never got a moment's peace. You said you were fed up with them. Don't you remember?"

Drusilla did not answer.

"I can understand that now," said Martin. "It must be terribly tiring being a mother."

"I trust I have always done my duty," said Drusilla in a huffy voice.

"Oh, yes, you have—of course you have," said Martin. "I just meant that children can be a bit of a nuisance. When they get bigger, I mean. Of course it's different when they're tiny babies, all pink and fat and blind and naked. They're really rather adorable then, don't you think?"

He half expected another sharp reply, but instead he noticed a dreamy look come over the face of his pet.

"Yes," murmured Drusilla. "Yes, they are."

"You can always have some more," said Martin.

The dreamy look promptly disappeared.

"Exactly how," said Drusilla acidly, "am I supposed to manage that? On my own?"

Martin looked puzzled. How her moods do change, he thought.

"You managed it before," he said.

"Martin," said Drusilla. "Didn't your mother ever teach you the facts of life?"

49

"I don't know what you mean," said Martin.

"It's high time you did," said Drusilla. "Listen to me."

Thus it came about that the very next morning, after the farmer had let his hens out into the orchard, Martin lay once more in ambush in the chicken house.

"Just get it firmly into your head," Drusilla had said, "that, for the reasons that I have explained to you, it's got to be a buck. And not just any old buck either—I shall not be best pleased if you bring home some toothless, doddering graybeard. But I shall be furious if you turn up with a doe. So make jolly sure you don't."

"But when I catch a mouse, Drusilla," said Martin, "how shall I know which it is?"

Drusilla gave a small squeak of annoyance. "Oh, I can't be bothered to go into all that now!" she said. "Just ask it. You've got a tongue in your head. Just say, 'Are you a buck?' "

I mustn't forget that, thought Martin now, and he practiced saying the words to himself. Then there was a scurrying sound overhead, and he looked up to see a mouse running along one of the perches, just above him. At sight of the kitten below it whisked around, twirling its long tail, and began to run back, but Martin was too quick for it. With one paw he cuffed it off the perch and with the other he pinned it down.

Bending his head, he spoke softly into its ear (for he had no wish to frighten it more than was necessary). "Are you a buck?" he said.

"No!" gasped the quivering mouse. "I'm a doe!"

"Oh, bother!" said Martin.

He lifted his paw.

"You're no good to me," he said. "I need a buck."

The mouse did not move. As Drusilla had once done, it lay staring at him as though mesmerized.

Poor little soul, thought Martin. "Cheer up!" he said. "My mistake!" He put on a jolly voice. " 'Beg your pardon, grant your grace, mind the cat don't scratch your face!' " he said heartily, and then he turned away and went back to his place of ambush.

Martin hunted all day, for he did not want to return to Drusilla empty-pawed, but strangely there seemed to be a great shortage of bucks. Little did he know that, once she had recovered, his first victim had been quick to spread the word through all the runways in the walls and the tunnels under the floor of the chicken house. "Pass it along," she had said to the first mouse she met, and soon all the buck mice in the place knew.

"If that crazy kitten should catch you," they said to one another, "just say you're a doe, and he'll let you go!"

51

"Sorry," said Martin to Drusilla that evening when he brought her a mouthful of corn from the hens' feeding trough, "I caught six altogether, but would you believe it, there wasn't a buck among them."

Drusilla stopped nibbling and looked up at him, her whiskers twitching.

"Strange," she said.

"Yes," said Martin. "Each one said, 'I'm a doe.' "

"You didn't let on that you were only after a buck, did you?"

"Well, yes. I did say that to the first one I caught."

"Ah!" said Drusilla. "I think maybe they were playing mouse-and-cat with you, Martin."

"How do you mean?"

"Pulling your leg."

"They never touched my leg," said Martin. "I don't get you."

"No," said Drusilla, "and you don't get me a husband either. I think we'll have to play things differently. Next mouse you catch, don't ask it anything. Simply bring it back here."

And the following morning Martin did. He caught a mouse—a big sleek dark one, it was—under the rabbit hutches and carried it back to the cart-shed, taking great pains not to be seen by any of his family. He bounded up the steps to the loft with it held carefully in his jaws and leaped onto the chest and looked down into the bathtub. He could not see Drusilla, but he supposed she must be inside the new nest that she had made from the fresh straw.

"Here you are, Drusilla!" cried Martin (indistinctly, as happens when people talk with their mouths full). "Is it a buck or a doe?"

But there was no answer.

8

Enough to make a cat laugh

Dropping into the bath (and dropping his new capture in it too), Martin cautiously pulled apart the nest ball of new straw.

There was nothing in it.

"Stay there!" said Martin to the sleek dark mouse (as if it had any choice), and leaping out again, he called Drusilla's name as loudly as he could.

From a far corner of the loft came two answers. One was the voice of his pet.

"Here, Martin, I'm here!" cried Drusilla faintly. "Oh, save me, save me!"

The other voice said no word. It just gave a low rumbling growl.

The semidarkness of the loft posed no problems for Martin, possessed, like all his race, with excellent night vision, and what he saw filled him with horror.

A few yards away, crouching between the legs of an old broken kitchen chair, was a very large cat, a cat far bigger than Robin or Lark or even Dulcie Maude. It was a cat that had been in a fair few fights, Martin could see by its battered ears, and because of these and because of its big round face he knew that it was a tom. Held beneath one of its forepaws was his pet.

For a moment he hesitated, fearing to tackle such an opponent, but then Drusilla cried once more, "Save me!" and he threw caution to the wind.

With a cry of "Leave my mouse alone!" Martin ran forward, only to receive a blow across the head that knocked him flying.

"*Your* mouse?" rumbled the big tomcat, his tail swishing. "You've got a nerve, young feller-me-lad. This mouse is mine, so clear out and let me eat it in peace."

"I'll tell my mother on you!" screamed Martin in a mixture of fright and hurt and impotent rage. "I'll tell my mother and she'll sort you out, you big ugly bully!"

"You watch your tongue," said the tom, "or it's you that'll get sorted out. Tell your mother indeed! Who's she anyway?"

"Her name's Dulcie Maude," yelled Martin, "and she could beat you with one paw tied behind her back!"

The look on the tom's face changed suddenly, from contemptuous anger to interested amusement.

"Well, well, well!" he said. "So you're Dulcie Maude's boy? In that case, I'll tell you what we'll do. We'll split this mouse, half each." And he bent his head toward Drusilla, ready to bite off hers.

In a fraction of a second, an idea flashed into Martin's mind. "Wait!" he screeched. "Don't eat that one! I've got another one, a bigger one. Have that instead."

The tom raised his head.

"Where is it then?" he said. "I don't see it."

"It's in the bathtub," Martin said.

"Just exactly what is going on, my lad?" said the tom. "I found this one in that tub."

"Well, that's where I keep my mice," said Martin.

"Keep them? Why not eat them straight off?"

"Oh, no," said Martin. "I keep them in the tub and I look after them and bring them lots of nice food."

"To fatten them up, you mean?" said the tom. "To make better eating?"

"Oh, no," said Martin. "I keep them as pets. I don't eat mice."

The tomcat was so astonished at this that he released his hold on Drusilla, who crawled dazedly to Martin and crept behind him for protection.

"This is my special pet, you see," said Martin, "and I've only just caught the one that's in the bath now, and he was going to be a husband for Drusilla if he's a he, which I don't know yet because Drusilla hasn't met him, and now she never will if you eat him, which I wish you wouldn't but I can't stop you, but if you try to get my Drusilla back I'll fight you until there isn't a breath left in my body!"

"I'm surprised there's one left now," said the tom, "after a speech like that."

He walked across the floor of the loft toward the bathtub and jumped up on the wooden chest and looked in. Martin, crouching protectively in front of Drusilla, could hear the scratch of little claws as the dark mouse skittered around the tub in helpless panic. Equally helplessly, Martin waited for the kill.

And even if he's satisfied and doesn't beat me up and then kill Drusilla as well, he thought, he'll be back, of course, now that he knows where to come.

But to his great surprise, the tomcat did not jump into the tub but back down onto the floor instead and came to sit beside him.

"You're a funny lad," he said. "What's your name?"

"Martin."

"I'm Pug. I expect that means something to you?"

"No," said Martin.

"Dulcie Maude's never mentioned me?"

"No."

"Typical," said Pug.

He stretched and yawned, and Drusilla, peeping around, shuddered at the sight of those claws and teeth.

"Go on, then," said Pug. "Stick her back in with the other one. There are plenty of other good mice on the farm."

"Do you mean . . . you're not going to kill either of them?" said Martin.

"No," said Pug. "You can keep your precious pets."

"I don't understand," said Martin, when he had carefully put Drusilla back in the tub. "Why have you spared their lives?"

"Because I like the look of you, young Martin," said Pug. "You're a strange boy—there's no getting away from that. Whoever heard of a kitten keeping mice as pets? It's enough to make a cat laugh! But you've got spirit, Martin, lad—I'll say that for you—you've got plenty of courage. If you fancy keeping pet mice, then you shall, and woe betide the cat that tries to stop you. I'm proud of you, my boy."

"I don't understand," said Martin again. "Why should you be?"

"Can't a father be proud of his son?" said Pug.

9

It was love at first sight

"You're my dad?" cried Martin.

"I'm your dad," said Pug. "By the way, how many brothers and sisters have you?"

"One of each."

"What color are they?"

"Well, Lark—she's tortoiseshell and white. Like Mother. And Robin—he's black."

"And you're a tabby. Like me."

"Yes, Dad." said Martin, feeling suddenly happy that it was so.

"And do they keep pet mice too?" said Pug.

"Oh, no," said Martin. "They're great mousers. Like Mother. And like you, I expect."

"You expect right, my son," said Pug. "Though actually I prefer rat-catching myself. More meat on 'em, you know. Ever thought of keeping a pet rat? I could soon pick one up for you."

"Oh, no thanks, Dad," said Martin. "I don't fancy them. It's mice I like. They're so little and pretty—especially Drusilla. And you should have seen her babies! They were so lovely when they were born, all pink and fat and blind and naked."

Pug licked his lips.

"What became of them?" he said.

"I let them go," said Martin, "when they were big enough. Drusilla asked me to. They were getting too much for her."

"And now she's asked you to find her a husband?"

"Yes."

"Typical," said Pug.

"Well, she explained it all to me, you see."

"Explained what?"

"About how you have to have a daddy as well as a mummy."

"Ah, yes," said Pug. "Just so. Well, now, we'd better go and see if you've picked the right kind for her."

"Wait a minute, Dad," said Martin hastily. "Let me go first. Let me explain things to them. Whichever the new one is, a buck or a doe, it'll have kittens if it suddenly sees you again."

"I see what you mean," said Pug. "I'll hold my horses, if you see what I mean."

Martin jumped up onto the chest. Already the nest

ball had been cobbled together again, and when he called her name, Drusilla came cautiously out of it.

"Has he gone?" she said.

"No," said Martin, "but it's all right, Drusilla—he won't hurt you."

"Won't hurt me! He was within an inch of biting my head off! Phew, I thought I was a goner!"

"Yes, but you'll be okay now. He's my father, you see, and he's agreed not to harm you—not to harm either of you. So tell me—did I choose right? Is it a buck?"

"Yes," said Drusilla.

"Oh, goody! But do you think you're going to like him? I can always change him."

"You'll do no such thing!" said Drusilla sharply.

She dropped her voice a little.

"Martin," she said, "he's the handsomest buck I ever saw. In fact," she whispered dreamily, "it was love at first sight."

How her moods do change, thought Martin.

"Ask him to come out, won't you?" he said. "And then I can show him to my father." And he called, "Dad!"

It took a little time for the sleek dark mouse to come out. Pug and Martin sat side by side and waited, while from inside the nest ball came the sound of muffled squeaks, as Drusilla strove to reassure the

newcomer. At last she persuaded him, and they sat looking up at the cats, Drusilla confidently now, the buck in some agitation.

"Hello, hello!" said Martin to him in a jolly voice. "Nice to see you again! Allow me to introduce my father, Mr. Pug. Now then, Dad, this is Drusilla . . ."

"We've already met," said Pug gravely.

". . . and this is . . . ?"

"Cuthbert," said Drusilla.

"Bert," gulped the dark mouse. "Call me Bert—all my pals do."

"Take no notice of him, Martin," said Drusilla. "His name is Cuthbert and Cuthbert he shall be called. It's a name of distinction, don't you agree, Mr. Pug?"

"Oh, certainly, Drusilla," said Pug.

"So let's hear no more of this 'Bert' nonsense," said

Drusilla firmly. "Is that understood, dear?"

"Oh, certainly, Drusilla," said Cuthbert.

Martin caught his father's eye. The look in it was one of rueful admiration.

"And now," said Drusilla, "I'm starving and so, I'm sure, is Cuthbert. So come along, Martin, don't just sit there. Stir your stumps and fetch us something really nice for supper."

"Oh, certainly, Drusilla," said Martin. "Are you coming, Dad?"

"No," said Pug. "You run along, Martin, lad. Stretch your legs. Get some fresh air. I'll mouse-sit for you, so you needn't worry about anything happening to these two."

But of course that was exactly what Martin did worry about. Already he had taken a great liking to his newfound father, but he didn't kid himself that Pug was anything other than a ruthless killer. Will he be able to keep his paws off my pets, he thought frantically as he hurried to find food for them. Let's hope they stay inside the nest till I get back or the mere sight of them might trigger him off. And the first thing he saw as he reentered the loft was his father sitting under the broken kitchen chair and licking a foot as though to clean it. To clean it of what? Blood?!

Martin dashed to the tub and peered in. There were Drusilla and Cuthbert, side by side, lapping daintily at a small pool of water.

Martin dropped in the food he was carrying and went to sit beside his father. The tomcat's big front paws, he could see, were soaking wet.

"Hello, Dad," he said. "Warm evening, isn't it? Been for a paddle?"

"They were thirsty," said Pug gruffly.

"But how did you know what to do?"

"She told me," said Pug.

Martin lay down and began to purr loudly with laughter.

"And you can wipe that grin off your face, my boy," said Pug, "or I'll wipe it off for you."

"Yes, Dad. Sorry, Dad," said Martin. "And Dad . . ."

"Well?"

"Thanks, Dad."

10

Mayday! Mayday!

During the next couple of weeks Pug paid a number of visits to the cart-shed loft to see this strange mouse-keeping son of his. Sometimes Martin was out, and then Pug would pass the time of day with Drusilla and Cuthbert. He was polite and seemed pleased to see them, the mice thought, though they noticed that he had a tendency to dribble.

During this time also, Drusilla grew noticeably fatter again.

"You're putting on weight, Drusilla," Martin said. "Am I overfeeding you?"

"Oh, for goodness' sake, Martin!" said Drusilla in her sharpest voice. "I thought I'd explained all that to you. Tell him, Cuthbert."

A look of smug self-satisfaction passed over Cuthbert's dark and handsome features.

"We are having a family," he said.

"Oh, of course!" said Martin. "How stupid of me! Congratulations, Cuthbert! What fun! When?"

"Quite soon," said Cuthbert. "In about another week, I think."

"Oh, good! Not long to wait," said Martin.

"Not long to wait, did you say?" said Drusilla in an icy voice. "Well, I do hope that both of you can manage to be patient. It must be such a trying time for you, sitting around waiting. Especially when I've got nothing at all to worry about except giving birth to umpteen babies in a cold hard prison—with primitive sanitation and very little privacy—from which there is no chance of escape. What a lucky mouse I am!"

"Typical," said Pug later, when Martin told him of Drusilla's outburst. "You save her from being eaten by me, you provide her with a husband, and you feed them both on the fat of the land. If that's not luck, I don't know what is."

"And she's going to have more babies," said Martin.

"Mm," said Pug. He licked his lips. "When?" he said.

"In about a week," said Martin. He looked narrowly at his father. "Dad!" he said. "You wouldn't . . . ?"

67

"No, no, Martin, lad," said Pug, "of course not, seeing that they're your pets. But all the same I think I'd better make myself scarce for a while. Out of temptation, you know. There's nothing quite as delicious as . . ."

"Stop!" cried Martin hurriedly. "I can't bear to think of such a thing. They're so little, so defenseless . . ."

". . . so tender," said Pug. "Just so."

He rose and stretched himself.

"See you around, my boy," he said. "Hope everything goes smoothly."

But it didn't.

The very next morning, not long after Martin had brought the mice a nice breakfast—pig feed for Cuthbert, and for Drusilla (who had grown strangely choosy in her likes and dislikes) a ripe strawberry stolen from the kitchen garden—he was sitting and chatting to his pets when they heard the sound of footsteps in the cart-shed below, and then the noise of barking, and then a human voice.

"What's all the fuss about, Bob?" said the farmer. "A cat up in the loft, is there?"

"There's a cat up in the loft!" raged Bob the collie dog. "Oh, if only I could get up these steps!"

"Don't worry about the dog," whispered Martin

up above. "He can't get up the steps."

"But the human can," said Drusilla. "And he'll be sure to find us. And then he'll kill me and my unborn children, fated now never to see the light of day!"

"What about me?" said Cuthbert.

"Oh, and you too, of course!" snapped Drusilla. "Hurry, Martin! You must get us out of this death trap."

Just then they heard the stairs creak as the farmer set foot on them.

Cuthbert's nerve broke.

"Mayday! Mayday!" he squeaked at the top of his voice.

"Listen to that!" grumbled the farmer as he climbed. "Blooming mice!"

Martin thought desperately. He could not carry both at once. There was only one decision.

69

"Women and children first!" he cried, and quick as a flash he jumped into the bathtub, picked up Drusilla, and leaped out again.

Hastily, and as gently as he could, he dropped her in a far dark corner of the loft and ran back for Cuthbert. But Cuthbert was still in a panic, scurrying round and round the tub squealing "Mayday!" in a quite hysterical way, and it took Martin a little while to get hold of him.

When at last he jumped out onto the wooden chest with Cuthbert in his mouth, the farmer was already in the loft.

"Bob was right!" he said. "There was a cat up here. And a proper little mouser too, by the look of it, like all Dulcie Maude's kittens. Good boy!"

He reached out to give the good boy a pat on the head.

Martin, thinking he was trying to take Cuthbert, growled fiercely.

Cuthbert, thinking the growl was directed at him, fainted clean away.

"That's one mouse less," said the farmer with satisfaction as he saw the body go limp in the kitten's jaws. "I'll leave you to eat it in peace." And he turned and climbed back down the steps.

Martin laid the unconscious Cuthbert down and began to lick his face in an attempt to revive him.

At this moment Drusilla reappeared, waddling awkwardly across the floor of the loft (for she was very heavy with young). From her hiding place she had heard the kitten growling, and now, to her horror, she saw that he was, it seemed, nuzzling at the dead body of her mate as cats often do prior to consuming their prey.

"Murderer!" she screamed. "You have made me a widow and orphaned my unborn children! You, who pretended to be my friend!" And she turned and staggered blindly away.

11

Number Eight

"Hang on, Drusilla!" cried Martin. "You've got it all wrong! Cuthbert's not dead, are you, Cuthbert?"

Or is he? thought Martin. Could he have died of fright?

"Speak to me, Cuthbert!" he cried.

But there was no reply.

Was it a heart attack perhaps? Had his heart stopped? How to restart it? He didn't know anything about first aid, but Drusilla would, competent and self-assured as always.

"Drusilla!" he shouted. "Come back! Cuthbert may need mouse-to-mouse resuscitation. Come here quickly!"

But there was no reply.

Leaving Cuthbert, Martin began to look frantically for Drusilla among all the heaps and piles of rubbish and junk that covered the corners of the loft floor. But he could not find her.

At last he returned to see how Cuthbert was faring.

But Cuthbert had gone.

For the rest of the morning Martin searched for his mice, calling their names in vain. Wherever they were (and there were so many nooks and crannies and hidey-holes in which they could be concealed), they kept silent.

Sadly he gave one last long look into the empty tub, scene of so many happy hours of conversation, birthplace of the first litter of cubs bred by the world's first mouse-breeding cat. Before long, he thought, Drusilla will have another lot of beautiful babies, all pink and fat and blind and naked. And I shall never see them, never watch them grow, never bring them their food and hear their squeaky little voices saying "Thank you, Uncle Martin."

I could catch another mouse, I suppose, and put it in the tub, but it wouldn't be the same. It couldn't be the same as my Drusilla.

He could not rid himself of the sound of her voice when last he had heard it, when she had called him a murderer, when she had cried so bitterly at him, "You, who pretended to be my friend!"

"I am your friend, Drusilla. I always will be," said Martin, but answer came there none, and, heavy hearted, he turned and left the loft.

For a while Martin returned each day, bringing offerings of food, which he left on the floor of the loft, but it was not touched. Drusilla and Cuthbert had emigrated. But where?

He made inquiries around the farm. "Have you seen my mice?" he asked, and got a variety of replies.

"Mice?" said a sheep (it may have been the same one he had met before—they all looked alike to him).

"Yes."

"Field mice?"

"Oh, don't start that again!" said Martin.

A cow that he asked simply said, "No." (It spoke with a broad accent so that the word sounded like "Noo"; perhaps it was "Moo," Martin thought later).

And when he went down to the pigsties and asked the boar, "Have you seen my mice?" the reply was "Oh, don't be such a bore!" (which puzzled Martin rather).

Disheartened, he decided to skip the farmer's daughter's pets (they'll only rabbit on at me, he thought) and, feeling thirsty, walked down to the duck pond for a drink. About the only good thing about losing his pets was that he needn't wet his feet anymore.

As he crouched and lapped, a duck swam near.

"Have you seen my mice?" said Martin.

"Didn't know you had a mice," quacked the duck.

"A mouse," said Martin. "Not a mice. You can't say 'a mice.' I had two of them."

"Two mouses?" said the duck.

"Oh, forget it!" said Martin crossly.

The duck shook its head and swam away, muttering "Mouses, mices, mices, mouses" to itself in a confused way.

Martin sat by the water's edge while the little ripples that the bird had made broke against the bank and gradually died away, leaving the surface of the pond glassy and still. Into this mirror he stared moodily, wondering what to do next. He closed his eyes the better to think, and when he opened them again, there were two reflections looking back at him from the mirror. Behind his own tabby face was a similarly marked but much larger one.

"Dad!" cried Martin.

"Hello, Martin, lad," said Pug. "Come to fetch a drink for your pets, have you?"

"Oh, no," said Martin. "They've gone, you see. I've lost them." And he told his father all that had happened.

"You haven't seen them, Dad, have you?"

"Not that I'm aware of," said Pug. "I don't actually inquire a mouse's name before I kill it, you know."

"So you could have . . . ?"

"No, no. I've been away. On business. Only just got back."

"Well, can you help me find Drusilla and Cuthbert? I've asked a number of different animals—a sheep, a cow, a pig, a duck—but none of them had anything sensible to say."

"You're asking the wrong creatures, my boy," said Pug. "If you want to find a mouse, ask another mouse. Go and catch one and ask it, that's my advice. I'll lend you a paw if you like. In fact, you'd better let me do the catching, it'll be quicker."

"But what if the mouse doesn't know where Drusilla is?"

"I'll eat it," said Pug simply. "Stay here. I won't be long."

And sure enough he was back in ten minutes with a mouse in his mouth. He dropped it in front of Martin, keeping one paw firmly on its tail to anchor it.

"Here's a young one for starters," said Pug. "Ask it."

"Don't be frightened," said Martin in a kindly voice to the terrified mouse. "We only want to ask you a simple question. Do you know where Drusilla lives?"

"Yes," whispered the young mouse.

"Where?"

"In a bathtub in the loft over the cart-shed."

"Wrong answer," said Pug. "You're out of date. And you're out of luck too."

"Wait, Dad, wait!" cried Martin, and to the mouse he said, "Why, you must be one of Drusilla's cubs, one of the eight that I released."

"I am, Uncle Martin, I am!" squeaked the young mouse desperately. "The smallest one, that said goodbye to you when you let me go, don't you remember?"

"Of course I do, kid!" said Martin excitedly. "I recognize you now. How you've grown! What are you, a buck or a doe?"

"A doe."

"How nice to see you again! How's life?"

"Almost at an end," said Pug.

"What are you called?" said Martin. "I forget."

"Eight," said the mouse. "Mother gave us all numbers, remember?"

"Come in, Number Eight," said Pug. "Your time is up." And he opened his mouth wide.

"No, Dad!" said Martin. "Please, this is one of my

mice. You mustn't eat her. She may be the very one to help me find her mother. You will, won't you, Eight?"

"Yes, Uncle Martin, oh, yes!" cried Eight.

"Promise?"

"Yes, yes, cross my heart!"

"And hope to die," said Pug dryly, "if you break your word." And he lifted his paw. "You're too soft, Martin lad," he said, as they watched Eight skipping thankfully away over the grass. "We'll never see her again."

But he was wrong.

12

Promises, promises

That very evening Martin was sitting outside the back door of the farmhouse, tidying himself up after a meal of fish-flavored Happipuss, when he heard a little voice say, "*Pssst!*"

He looked about him and saw Eight peeping around the edge of a trash can.

Martin had the sense to say nothing, for Dulcie Maude and Robin and Lark were all nearby. Instead he walked slowly away, hoping that Eight would follow. He made for the Dutch barn, thinking that if they should be interrupted, the little mouse could hide among the straw.

Martin lay down upon a bale at the foot of the stack and waited, and before long there was a rustling and Eight appeared beside him.

"I've found Mother, Uncle Martin," she said.

"Good kid!" said Martin. "And Cuthbert?"

"Who's Cuthbert?"

"Her husband. A dark handsome fellow."

"Oh, is that what he's called?" said Eight. "Yes, he was there. Mother just said to me, 'Eight, this is your stepfather.' He seemed very nervous."

"He is rather highly strung," said Martin. "But they were both well, I trust?"

"Oh, yes."

"And the new babies? She had the babies all right?"

"Yes. Twelve."

"Twelve!" said Martin. "Goodness me, she's got them numbered up to twenty now then?"

"No," said Eight. "These are all called after the months of the year. It worked out nicely, Mother said, because they're mostly bucks. Only three does—April, May, and June."

"How charming!" said Martin. "I can't wait to see them!"

"Well, that's just it, Uncle Martin," said Eight nervously. "You can't."

"Why not? You've only got to tell me where they are."

"I can't."

"Why not?"

"She made me swear not to tell you. She said you'd only put them all back in the bathtub."

"I wouldn't, honest, I wouldn't!" cried Martin.

"You must take me to her, Eight, so that I can tell her so myself. You promised you'd help me find her."

"I know," said Eight unhappily, "but now I've had to promise Mother I won't. I know you'll be angry with me, Uncle Martin, but what am I to do?"

"I shan't be angry, Eight," said Martin, "but I'll tell you who will be if he finds out."

"Your father?"

"Yes," said Martin. "He'll kill you for sure."

At that moment they heard the smallest of sounds somewhere high above them on top of the stack of bales, and a corn stalk floated down and landed beside them. Eight jumped in fright, but Martin said, "Don't be scared. It's only a straw in the wind. Probably a bird messing around. Now listen, Eight. I understand the fix you're in, but I want you to do one more thing for me. Go back to Drusilla and tell her I won't put them all back in the tub. Tell her I promise not to. Say that I just want to see her again, and Cuthbert, and the babies. Say I miss her very much. And then come back and tell me what she says. Will you do that for me?"

Eight looked doubtful.

"But you'll see where I'm going, Uncle Martin," she said, "and then you'll follow me and then you'll find them and then Mother will never forgive me."

"Look," said Martin, "I won't follow you. I'll go right down to the other end of the farmyard, and I'll shut my eyes and count to a hundred."

"Promise?" said Eight.

"I promise," said Martin. "And you'll come back and find me and tell me what Drusilla said?"

"All right."

"Promise?" said Martin.

"I promise," said Eight.

So off went Martin in one direction, and after a while, off went Eight in another.

"Promises, promises!" growled a deep voice on top of the stack of bales, and off went Pug. After Eight.

13

You must be joking!

All that night Martin wandered around the farmyard, calling every now and then in the hope that Eight would hear his voice and run to him with news. But she did not appear.

Instead, his mother came upon him as he sat on the wall of the pigsties, mewing, and scolded him for making so much noise.

"Stop that caterwauling at once, Martin!" she hissed. "How on earth do you expect to catch mice if you advertise your presence like that? Quite apart from the fact that you'll spoil the night's hunting for the rest of us—for me and for Robin and Lark."

"And Dad," said Martin.

"Your father?" said Dulcie Maude. "When did you last see your father?"

"Yesterday."

"Hm," said Dulcie Maude. "I did not know that you were acquainted with him."

"Oh, yes. Actually he's only just got back. He's been away. On business."

"Pah!" spat Dulcie Maude angrily, and she stalked off, lashing her tail.

"Typical," said a voice behind Martin, a voice that was familiar yet strangely muffled.

Martin looked around to see Pug with a small mouse in his mouth. It was Eight!

"Dad!" he cried. "You haven't . . . ?"

Pug put Eight carefully down on the ground.

"Keep your hair on, Martin, lad," he said.

Eight squeaked, "It's all right, Uncle Martin, Mr. Pug was kindly giving me a lift."

"Good job I did, young lady," growled Pug. "or you'd have walked straight down Dulcie Maude's throat."

"Heard you talking in the Dutch barn, you see," he said to Martin. "So I followed her. Just in case she didn't come back to tell you what your precious Drusilla said."

"I would have done, I would have done, Mr. Pug!" cried Eight. "I promised!"

"Yes, yes, all right," said Pug. "No need to sound so hurt. You haven't been."

"But what *did* Drusilla say?" said Martin.

"Mother doesn't want to see you again, Uncle Martin," said Eight. "She says she's sure you mean well, but she's not taking any chances. 'Once a pet-keeper, always a pet-keeper,' she said. 'I feel bad about it,' she said, 'because I owe my life to Martin, but I can't risk it. Maybe he wouldn't put us back in the tub,' she said, 'but he might get some other crazy idea for keeping us, and I value my freedom too much.' " Eight paused for breath.

"Oh," said Martin.

"I'm sorry, Uncle Martin," said Eight.

"Didn't she even send a message?" asked Martin miserably.

"She sent her best regards."

"Oh," said Martin. "Well, that's nice, I suppose."

"You run along home now, young Eight," said Pug. "And mind how you go."

"Yes, Mr. Pug," said Eight, "and thanks for the lift." And she scuttled away into the darkness.

"But, Dad," said Martin, "You must know where Drusilla and her family are. You followed Eight there, so you must know."

"I do, Martin, lad," said his father, "but I'm not telling you. I've gone along with you so far, but now I think it's high time you forgot all about this silly business of keeping mice as pets. You heard what

Drusilla said—it's her freedom that she values. It's all very well humans keeping tame animals as pets, like those rabbits, which have never known any other sort of life. But to keep a wild animal like a mouse shut up—it's wrong, you know. Just think how lucky you are, to be free to go where you like and do what you want."

"But I'm not wild, Dad."

"All cats are wild at heart, my son. Many are lucky, especially farm cats like us, but some town cats are nothing better than prisoners, kept indoors all the time. Well treated, maybe, well fed and fussed over, but just as much prisoners as those rabbits. You don't know how lucky you are. What if some humans came out here from the town one day to buy some free-range eggs?"

"Well?"

"What if they bought a free-range tabby kitten as well?" said Pug. "And took it away with them to a new home? Just imagine," he said, warming to his work, "this tabby kitten, who's been used to going where he likes and doing what he wants out in the fresh air of the countryside, suddenly becomes a town cat. He's shut up all day in a house—no, an apartment, more likely—yes, a shabby little apartment right up at the top of a high-rise, miles from the ground."

"He's not a free-range tabby kitten any longer. Not free to walk in the woods and the fields. Not even free to dig a nice hole in the flower bed to make himself comfortable—all he'll have is a box full of cat litter. He's just a *pet*"—Pug spat the word—"an imprisoned pet, probably belonging to some ghastly little girl who'll be forever picking him up and cuddling him and kissing him with her horrible slobbery mouth. And to crown it all, she'll very likely tie a big blue silk bow around the wretched creature's neck!"

"Oh, Dad!" said Martin. "You must be joking!"

14

Escape

This is no joke, thought Martin, as he tried unsuc-cessfully with one hind foot to scratch off the big silk bow that was tied around his neck. It was a yellow bow, to be sure—not a blue one—put there not by a little girl but by a large lady, but otherwise most of what Pug had said had actually happened.

A number of people had come out to the farm, as they did at weekends to buy fresh milk and new-laid eggs, and Martin (I should have had more sense! he thought now angrily) had wandered among them, daydreaming about his precious Drusilla, his father's warning entirely forgotten.

Suddenly a hand had scooped him up, and he found himself pressed to the large bosom of a large lady.

"Oh, what a sweet little kitty!" she cried, and to the farmer's wife she said, "I don't suppose you'd consider selling her, would you? She's so pretty, I've fallen in love with her, love at first sight!"

"Well, I don't know," said the farmer's wife. "I'll have to ask my husband."

"It's a he anyway, not a she," said the farmer's daughter in the scornful tone that countryfolk use to townspeople who can't tell the difference between a bull and a cow.

"And a proper little mouser he is too," said the farmer. "Saw him only the other day with a big one in his mouth."

"Oh, goodness me, we don't have mice," said the large lady in the scornful tone that townspeople use to countryfolk who can't keep vermin out of their houses. "I just want him for a pet."

Of course, none of this conversation meant anything to Martin. All he knew was that the large lady produced some cash and the farmer's wife produced a box and popped him into it and closed the lid.

I should have had more sense, thought Martin once more, as he scrabbled at the yellow ribbon. "I told you so"—that's what Dad would say. He stared out of the fourth-floor window at the street far below and the view of houses and yet more houses, and mewed with misery at the thought that he would never see his father again. Or his mother. Even seeing Robin and Lark would be a pleasure.

He looked around the room. Though much more luxurious, it was as much a prison as the tub had been for Drusilla. He looked at the comfortable chairs whose cushions he must not knead and whose covers he must not scratch (he had learned), at the heavy curtains at which he must not bite (he had learned), and at the thick pale wall-to-wall carpeting, which to dirty in any way would be unthinkable (this he had not needed to learn, being clean by nature). The box full of cat litter stood in a corner, just as Pug had said it would. He looked at the closed door. Once or twice he had slipped through it, but it only led to other rooms with other doors. And the window was closed and latched.

There was no escape.

Escape now occupied all Martin's thoughts. It wasn't that the large lady treated him unkindly. On the contrary, she spoiled him rotten. She bought him a beautiful wickerwork satin-lined cat bed, and she fed him royally. Ordinary cat food was not good enough for her precious pet; he must have steak and chicken breast and Gold Top milk to drink. And she was forever cooing and gooing over him and stroking and smoothing his coat, to which Martin made no objection but purred automatically at these attentions.

But all the time he was thinking of the farm, of his family, of Drusilla, of freedom.

For a human prisoner to escape from confinement, a lot of planning is usually needed: a file, for example, must be smuggled in for cutting through the bars of a window, an impression secretly taken of a key and a duplicate made, a tunnel dug, or a ladder built.

But sometimes there are moments when the prisoner has made no plan at all but simply seizes an unexpected opportunity when it occurs: a working crew, for instance, is out on the moors when suddenly a blanket of mist descends upon convicts and warders alike, and a man who minutes before had not imagined doing any such thing slips away into the murk.

So it befell with Martin.

It was a hot morning, and the person who came to clean the large lady's apartment put down her duster and said to Martin, "Phew! It's stuffy in here, isn't it, puss? Let's have a bit of fresh air." And she opened the window before going on with her dusting.

Martin jumped up onto the windowsill. Now that he could look straight down, he saw that the ground was a very long way away, so far that any cat foolish enough to try to reach it would without doubt use up all its nine lives in one go. But he also noticed something else, something that he had not properly appreciated when staring through the glass of the closed window. There was a tree below too.

It was quite a large tree, its crown almost as high as the third floor of the high-rise, so that a really desperate kitten (which he was not) just might with a wild leap be able to launch itself outward into the leafy top and survive. But there was one branch, Martin could now see, which stuck out at such an angle that a really brave kitten (which he was) could—if he judged it correctly—drop from the windowsill onto it.

If he miscalculated, if his aim was even the slightest bit wrong, that would be dead wrong.

"Right!" said the cleaner. "That's the dusting done, puss. I'll fetch the Hoover."

Martin tensed himself.

Then he let himself fall from the sill, legs spread wide, paws opened wide, claws unsheathed, tail whipping madly around, eyes fixed upon the branch below.

15

Alec Smart

Now there occurred a nightmare procession of close shaves for Martin.

First, because the tree was swaying a little in the breeze, he failed to make a perfect landing on the branch, but half slid off it, scrambling madly to keep his balance; as he did so, one end of the yellow silk around his throat caught on a projecting twig, and at the same time Martin lost his grip and fell.

For an awful moment he hung by his neck, swinging to and fro and choking for breath. Then, because it was a bow, the knot undid itself, and he dropped the rest of the way to the ground.

No sooner had he landed, dazed and gasping, than he heard a loud barking, and a large hairy dog came rushing toward him.

Wildly Martin dashed across the road, almost under the wheels of a passing car, and in through the nearest gateway he could see. He ran along a path by the side of a house and found himself in a garden, at the bottom end of which was a shed. Under the shed was a space, and into this Martin crept and lay panting.

At first he was too busy catching his breath to notice, but gradually he became aware of a strange smell. It was a vaguely familiar smell that he had caught little whiffs of before, on the farm, around the chicken house and the shed where the ducks were shut at nights, but here it was very strong.

"Good afternoon," said a voice suddenly.

It was a sharp, rather nasal voice, and, peering through the gloom under the floor of the shed, Martin could see a sharp long-nosed face staring at him.

"Good afternoon," said the fox once more, "or do you not think that this afternoon is good?"

Martin found his tongue.

"No," he said, "no, I don't. You see, I've just jumped out of a fourth-floor window and nearly hanged myself on a tree and almost been chewed up by a large hairy dog and narrowly missed being run over by a car and now . . ."

". . . and now you think you're going to be eaten by a fox."

"I hope not," said Martin in a small choked voice.

"You're not," said the fox. "We don't. I'm afraid we don't care for the smell of cats."

Martin could not think of anything to say to this, in view of the awful rank stink with which the air was filled, so he said nothing.

"What's your name?" said the fox.

"Martin."

"Mine's Smart. Alec Smart. Anyway, what have you been up to, Martin? Sounds like you've used up four of your nine lives in one day."

"I'm trying to get home, Mr. Smart," said Martin.

"Call me Alec. Where's home?"

"I live on a farm, Alec."

"What are you doing in the middle of the town, then?"

"A lady came to the farm and took me away in a box."

"You were kitnapped," said Alec Smart, grinning. "And now you've escaped. Whereabouts is this farm of yours?"

"I don't know."

"Well, I'm acquainted with most of the farms around this town. Tell me something about it."

"It's got cows and pigs and sheep and hens and

ducks and a black-and-white collie dog. And cats of course, my family."

"Big deal," said the fox. "Could be any one of a dozen."

"Oh, and there are some rabbits," said Martin. "Three big white rabbits with pink eyes who live in three hutches at the bottom of the garden."

"Now you're talking," said Alec. "Not every farm would have them. Tell you what, I'm not doing anything particular tonight. I'll pop out of town and have a look around if you like. Haven't had a night out in the country for ages. I could do with a breath of fresh air."

So could I, thought Martin, wrinkling his nose.

"It's very kind of you, Alec," he said.

"Think nothing of it," said the fox. "White rabbits, did you say?"

"Yes."

"Big ones?"

"Yes."

"With pink eyes?"

"Yes."

"Three of them?"

"Yes," said Martin. "Do you think that that information would help you to find my farm?"

"It certainly gives me something to get my teeth

into," said the fox. He yawned, showing a lot of sharp ones.

"Time I got a bit of shut-eye," he said. "And you must be tired after all that dicing with death. Why don't you take a catnap?"

I couldn't sleep under here, thought Martin, not in this stink.

And as if reading his mind Alec Smart said, "Jump upon the roof of the shed. It's a nice day—you could do a bit of sunbathing."

"Yes, right, Alec," said Martin. "I will."

"By the way," said Alec, "before I forget. Supper is served every evening at dusk. Over in that corner, by the woodpile."

"Supper?"

"Two saucerfuls. One of milk, one of Champion Bow-Wow."

"You mean the humans who live here actually feed you?"

"They do," said Alec, "though they believe they are feeding a hedgehog that lives in the woodpile. After they put the food down, just wait till they've gone and then help yourself."

"But what about you?"

"Oh, I shall eat out tonight," said Alec. "Grab myself some takeout."

"Doesn't the hedgehog ever get what they put out?" asked Martin.

"He does not," said Alec. "He knows better. It's a protection racket, you see."

"What does that mean?"

"A little business arrangement between me and my spiny friend. I get his milk and his meat."

"And what does he get?"

"He," said Alec Smart, "gets his life. He owes it to me. I spared it."

"How?"

"Caught him one night as he crossed the lawn. Tipped him over on his back."

"Why?"

"Always bite a hedgehog in the belly," said Alec, "unless you want a prickle sandwich. As I was saying, I tipped him over and I was just going to unzip him when he squealed out, 'Mercy! Mercy!' "

Oh, thought Martin, oh, Drusilla! The first words you ever spoke to me!

"So you spared his life!" Martin said. "How good of you, Alec!"

"Wasn't good at all," said the fox, "it was quick thinking. No more hedgehog, no more food put out. 'Get this, piggy,' I said to him, 'from now on what's yours is mine. Just let me catch you with your snout in one of those saucers and you're a goner, understand?' 'Oh, yes, sir, yes, sir,' he said. 'I'll never touch a mouthful again.' And he never has."

"But the people still think that he's eating what they put out?"

"They do," said Alec. "Very easily tricked, you see, humans are. They know that whenever a hedgehog has finished eating or drinking out of a saucer, it always turns it upside-down in case there's a worm or a beetle underneath it. So when you've finished tonight, remember to tip the dishes over."

All that afternoon Martin slept on the sun-warmed roof of the garden shed. He woke at twilight when a woman came across the lawn carrying two saucers and put them down by the woodpile.

Martin waited until she had gone back into her house, and then he got to his feet and stretched himself. He jumped down and looked into the space beneath the shed.

"Alec?" he called, but there was no answer, so he walked across and polished off the milk and the Champion Bow-Wow, remembering to tip both saucers upside-down afterward.

What a cunning fellow that fox is, he thought as he sat by the woodpile cleaning his face. If anyone can find the way to my farm it's old Alec Smart.

16

All the smells of home

What a cunning fellow I am, said Alec to himself. He stared hungrily at the three rabbit hutches at the bottom of the garden. This was Martin's farm, all right. Already the fox had visited a number of others, quickly, efficiently, not allowing himself to be distracted by thoughts of hens or ducks or geese or turkeys. He simply checked to see that there were no rabbit hutches in each garden, and then moved on, loping easily across the fields.

Now here was journey's end.

The moon was shining brilliantly, and as he padded down the lawn he could see three pairs of eyes shining red in its glow. For a few seconds the rabbits stared in horror before each whisked into its sleeping compartment.

Alec Smart drew nearer. He had much experience with rabbit hutches and he knew they were of two kinds. One kind had doors you could open. The other had doors you could not. It all depended on the way they were secured.

A bolt was very difficult to undo (Alec had even met hutch doors that were padlocked and these of course were impossible), and hook-and-eye catches were tricky. Turn buttons were the easiest fastenings to undo, especially if they were big oblong wooden ones. Like these. You could turn them with your nose or your paw and then the doors of the hutch would swing open.

"Now," said Alec, "which one of you shall I invite to join me for supper tonight?" He sat down and began to chant, "Eenie meenie minie mo, catch a bunny by its toe . . ." but at the sound of his voice all three rabbits began to stamp with their hind feet on the floorboards of their sleeping compartments, making quite a loud tattoo in the silent garden.

Alec stopped his chanting as these warning signals rang out and, choosing the middle hutch, began to scratch with one paw at a turn button. It was stiff, so that he could not shift it easily, and he was just about to try another when, in an interval in the rabbits' drumming, he suddenly heard a quite different noise. It was a kind of rasping singsong, rising and falling in a way that sounded unpleasantly threatening.

Alec spun around, and there behind him, crouched

flat upon the grass, its tail twitching, its battered ears flat above its big round tom's face, was a very large tabby cat.

Instantly the fox too flattened his ears, while the hair on his red coat rose and he fluffed out his brush. He drew back his lips from his teeth in a silent grimace.

For a moment there was no sound in the garden but

the stamping of the rabbits, and then: "Beat it, stinker!" growled Pug, rising to his full height.

"Who are you calling stinker?" snarled Alec.

"You," said Pug. He stepped one inch nearer to the fox.

"I'm going to have to teach you some manners," said Alec. He stepped back two inches.

"Just you try it," said Pug, advancing four inches.

"You come any closer and I will," said Alec, retreating eight inches. This brought his backside up against the trestle on which the rabbit hutches stood.

In fact, Alec had no wish to tangle with such an ugly-looking customer, so now he braced himself to leap clean over the tomcat and take his leave, with as much dignity as possible.

Just then the cat raised his big round head and stared over the fox's head, as though he were looking at something above and behind him.

The oldest trick in the world, thought Alec. He's pretending there's something behind me and, when I turn to look, he'll rush me. I'm not falling for that one, not likely.

Next instant something dropped from the roof of one of the hutches, dropped squarely onto the fox's back and dug into it an awful lot of sharp claws, and at the same time the tomcat let out an earsplitting yowl and charged.

Alec Smart fled, with no dignity at all.

"Well done, old girl," said Pug to Dulcie Maude. "I just wish Martin had been here to see you in action!"

"You and your precious Martin," said Dulcie Maude. "I've never known you to take such a liking to one of our children before."

"I never have," said Pug quietly. "I miss him."

"Well, you'd better get over it," said Dulcie Maude. "You're never going to see him again."

"Nice to see you again!" called Martin from the roof of the shed, as Alec came slinking in in the gray dawn. He jumped down to greet the fox.

"You look bushed," he said.

"I am," said Alec.

"And your back—it's all scratched! What happened

to it? Did you catch it under a barbed-wire fence?"

"You could say that."

"Did you find my farm? With the three rabbits at the bottom of the garden?"

"I did, Martin, I did."

"You didn't hurt the rabbits, did you, Alec?"

"Oh, no," said the fox. "Never harmed a hair of their heads. As if I would."

"Did you meet my dad?"

"Your dad?"

"He's big, and the same color as me."

"With rather battered ears?"

"Yes."

"I did, Martin, I did."

"How did you get along with him?"

"We exchanged a few words."

"And my mother—did you see her?"

"Just a glimpse."

"How did she strike you?"

"Unexpectedly," said Alec.

"How do you mean?"

"She came as quite a surprise to me."

"Did you tell them that I was coming home?"

"Actually, no."

"Good," said Martin. "It'll be quite a surprise to them, then. When can we start?"

"Not till tonight," said Alec firmly. "I am footsore and weary and I need a good day's sleep." And he crawled under the shed.

How the hours dragged by for Martin. At long last it was dusk, and the hedgehog's supper was put out.

Martin was looking at it longingly when the fox appeared.

"We'll split it," he said. "You have the milk and I'll have the meat. After all, you'll soon be back on your farm, and farms are always riddled with mice. I bet you're fond of a nice fat mouse, eh?"

"Yes," said Martin, lapping at the milk.

I *am* fond of a nice fat mouse, he thought with a sigh, and her name is Drusilla and I don't suppose I'll ever see her again because she's afraid I'll shut her up, which I won't because now I know what it's like to be a prisoner.

"Can we go now?" he said.

"Not till the small hours," said Alec. "Too many people still around, and too much traffic." And he disappeared through the hedge.

So Martin waited, as patiently as he could, until at last a familiar stink told him of the fox's return.

Out of town they went, hurrying along the deserted streets, and the fox led the kitten across country until at last they came to the edge of a wood on the crest of a little hill. The moonlight showed a cluster of buildings in the valley below.

"That's it," said Alec, and "That's it!" cried Martin excitedly. "I can smell all the smells of home!"

The fox lifted his muzzle to the wind, sifting the messages it brought and noting in particular the scent of chickens.

"Off you go then, Martin," he said.

"Aren't you coming?"

"Not just now. But I might drop in one of these nights," said Alec Smart, and he turned and melted away into the darkness of the wood.

"Thanks for everything, Alec!" called Martin after him.

He lay for a little while, savoring his homecoming. Night was changing to day, and in the trees behind him the birds began their dawn chorus. Down at the farm the first cock crowed and as though in answer there sounded from the far end of the wood the sharp yap of a fox.

Martin rose to his feet and trotted happily home.

17

He brought me a strawberry once

From the top of the hill, Martin had had a bird's-eye view of the farm. Now, lower down, he had a cat's-eye view but one that he had never seen before. His kittenhood had been spent entirely within the main cluster of buildings—the farmhouse, the cowsheds, the pigsties, the poultry houses, the Dutch barn, and, of course, the old cart-shed with its loft.

Now, approaching home from the outside for the first time, he noticed that there was another quite isolated building, a long low open-fronted shed, used to provide shelter for outlying cattle in wintertime. It was a couple of fields away from the farmyard, and he had not even known of its existence.

Curious (like all his kind), Martin went to explore it. Daintily (like all his kind), he picked his way over the crust of dried mud and dung in front of the shed and looked in. There was some moldy hay in the row of wooden mangers that lined the back wall, and the earthen floor had a thin cover of musty straw, but there was no sign of life. No sign of life, that is, until suddenly Martin saw a movement in the straw in front of him and quickly and instinctively (like all his kind) pounced. A squeak of terror told him, as did his nose, that he had caught a mouse, and though his first impulse was to let the wretched thing go, he decided on second thought to question it. You never could tell, it just might know where Drusilla was.

He pulled the mouse carefully from beneath the straw and examined it. It was a big sleek dark one. It was Cuthbert!

"Cuthbert!" cried Martin in high delight. "It's me, Martin!"

Cuthbert fainted clean away.

Visions of Cuthbert's last faint flashed through Martin's mind. How he had tried to revive him. How Drusilla had screamed at him and called him a murderer. "You, who pretended to be my friend!" were the last words she had spoken to him.

At that instant he heard her voice again.

"Cuthbert?" she called. "Did you squeak?"

Quick as a flash, Martin leaped up into the nearest manger and hid behind the moldy hay. Peering through it, he saw Drusilla come out of a hole in the wall. She waddled awkwardly across the floor of the shed (for she was—once again—very heavy with young) until she reached Cuthbert, who opened his eyes and got dazedly to his feet.

"Where is he?" he said.

"Where is who?"

"Martin."

"Martin? You know quite well where Martin is, Cuthbert," said Drusilla sharply. "Mr. Pug told us, weeks ago. He's gone to live in town."

"Well, he's back," said Cuthbert. "He just caught me. Didn't you hear me squeak?"

"You were dreaming," said Drusilla. "You were squawking in your sleep. I saw you, lying there with your eyes shut."

"I was pretending," said Cuthbert hastily. "I was

114

pretending to be dead. Playing possum. So as to fool him."

"Of course," said Drusilla. "Of course."

She did not love her handsome husband the less for knowing that he was an extremely nervous person. But for long now she had felt guilty about Martin. She had called him a murderer. Poor boy.

"Are you certain it was really Martin, Cuthbert?" she said.

"Quite certain."

"He brought me a strawberry once," said Drusilla dreamily. "When I was pregnant with the Months, do you remember?"

Drusilla usually referred to her firstborn brood of children collectively as the Numbers and to the second litter as the Months, all of whom—the nine boys plus April, May, and June—had now left home. What she would call the coming litter would depend on their quantity.

"Yes, I remember," said Cuthbert, "but it's long past strawberry time now."

"More's the pity. I really fancy fresh fruit just now. A lovely juicy ripe blackberry from that bush in the farm garden—that would be yummy," said Drusilla, and she waddled off back to her hole. Cuthbert followed, casting wary glances about him.

Martin lay in the manger for a while, savoring

what he had just overheard. She had spoken quite kindly of him! She should have her blackberry!

He jumped down and set off for the farm.

How would his family feel, he wondered, to see him back again?

He soon found out.

By this time, with nothing but a dishful of hedgehog's milk inside him and that many hours ago, Martin was not only thirsty again but very hungry.

First he went to the duck pond for a drink. The farmer was already driving the cows in for milking, but the ducks had not yet been let out, and the pond was still and mirrorlike. Martin, crouching at the

He brought me a strawberry once

edge to lap, saw not only his own reflection but also that of another cat. Because of its tortoiseshell-and-white coloring he thought at first that it was his mother, but then he heard Lark's voice.

"Look who's here!" she sneered. "It's the wimp! Going paddling, wimp, are you?"

How she's grown, thought Martin, and then he looked closely into the mirror and saw that he too had grown, even more. He was quite a big cat. He was quite an angry cat too, he discovered, who did not like being spoken to in that manner, and he whipped around and hit his sister such a smack across the nose that she ran off yowling.

Martin took a long satisfying drink, and then he went to the backdoor of the farmhouse, where the farmer's wife had not long since put out a dish of chicken-flavored Happipuss. Hardly had he taken a mouthful when he heard behind him the voice of his brother.

"Look who's here!" sneered Robin. "It's the wimp! Clear off, wimp, and leave that meat alone!"

Martin said nothing. He simply turned around, slowly, and began to move, very slowly, toward his brother. He flattened his ears and drew back his lips from his teeth and inched, very, very slowly, forward, until the tabby head and the black head were almost touching. All the time he was making a kind of rasping singsong, rising and falling in a way that sounded unpleasantly threatening.

Robin's nerve broke, and he fled.

Martin enjoyed a long satisfying meal and went down to the garden to inspect the blackberry bush. The farmer's daughter had just fed her rabbits, and as she went back into the farmhouse, Dulcie Maude came out of it.

Martin walked past the rabbit hutches (where there was a lingering smell of fox) and was busy looking for a really juicy blackberry when he heard his mother's voice.

"Martin!" she said sharply.

"Yes, Mother?"

"Where on earth have you sprung from? Why have you come home? Why are you eating blackberries, eh? Why aren't you catching mice, like an ordinary normal cat?"

"Because, Mother," said Martin firmly, "I am not an ordinary normal cat."

"You can say that again!" said Dulcie Maude.

Martin said it again.

"Pah!" spat Dulcie Maude angrily, and she stalked off, lashing her tail.

"Typical," said a familiar voice.

"Dad!" cried Martin, and "Martin, lad!" growled Pug, and they rubbed their round tabby faces together, purring with simple happiness.

"How did you find your way home?" Pug asked, and Martin told him all about his adventures and his escape and how a kindly fox had guided him home.

"A fox, eh?" said Pug.

"Yes and, Dad, he got his back quite nastily scratched, too."

"Did he?" said Pug. "Well, well."

"And, Dad," said Martin excitedly, "I've found Drusilla and Cuthbert!"

"Ah, you came back that way? Past the field shed?"

"Yes. They should be pretty safe right out there, shouldn't they?"

"They are quite safe," said Pug. "I have made it perfectly plain to the rest of the family that the field shed is my territory, not to be trespassed upon."

"You hunt there?"

"Yes."

"But not . . . ?"

"No, no, not your precious Drusilla and her husband."

"But what about all their children? What about Eight?"

"No, Eight's quite safe. Married a nice young chap from the pigsties. Living down there now. Going to have babies of her own."

"Gosh!" said Martin. "Drusilla a grandmother! Imagine! But how do you mean, she's safe? Mother might catch her, or Robin or Lark."

"She has to take her chance on that, Martin," said Pug. "At least she's in no danger from me. I've given her a password and told her to tell it to all Drusilla's other children. Then, if I catch them, they shout it out, and I let 'em go."

"What's the password?"

" 'Martin's Mice!' Caught a youngster in the chicken house the other day and I was just going to bite his head off when he squeaked, 'Martin's Mice!' 'That was a narrow squeak,' I said to him. 'What's your name?' I said. 'March,' he said. 'Well, quick march,' I said, 'and don't let me catch you in here again.' I sometimes wish I hadn't thought of the password idea. Amazing number of mice seem to have belonged to you."

"I shan't ever keep any more, Dad," said Martin, "now that I know what it's like to be shut up. But I'd like to keep in touch with them. Can we go over to the field shed now? Drusilla fancies a nice blackberry, you see." And he put his face up and carefully mouthed off a large dark fruit.

Father and son walked together across the dewy fields in the morning sunshine. They were silent, Martin because his mouth was full, Pug because he was simply enjoying the return of his favorite, but when they came near to the shed he said, "You go on alone, Martin, lad. She'll like to see you by yourself. I'll join you later," and he lay down in the grass.

Martin walked quietly into the open-fronted shed and sat beside the hole down which he had seen Drusilla disappear. He placed the blackberry on the floor in front of him.

"Drusilla!" he called softly.

From the depths of the hole came a squeak and then silence. That's Cuthbert, thought Martin. Hope he hasn't fainted again.

He called once more, and after a little while a familiar face appeared in the mouth of the hole.

"Hello, Drusilla," said Martin. "I hear you're expecting another happy event. Many congratulations! I'm sure you'll be glad when it's all over—it must be so tiring for you. I don't know if you'd like it, but I've brought you a nice fresh juicy blackberry."

Drusilla squeezed herself out of the hole.

"Oh, Martin!" she said. "There never was a cat like you!"